For Mum and Dad.
N.P.

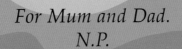

Copyright © 2002 by Nik Pollard

Published by Roaring Brook Press
A division of The Millbrook Press, 2 Old New Milford Road, Brookfield, Connecticut 06804.
First published in the United Kingdom by David Bennett Books Limited in 2002.

Library of Congress Cataloging-in-Publication Data

Pollard, Nik.
The Tide / Nik Pollard.
p. cm.
Summary: Describes the sights and sounds at the seashore and the cyclical nature of the tides.
[1. Tides—Fiction. 2. Seashore—Fiction. 3. Seashore animals—Fiction.] I. Title.

PZ7.P7583 Ti 2002
[E]—dc21

ISBN 0-7613-1536-5 (trade edition)
0-7613-2467-4 (library binding)

Printed in China

10 9 8 7 6 5 4 3 2 1
First American edition 2002

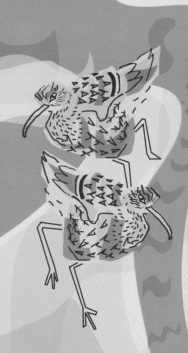

The Tide

nik Pollard

Roaring Brook Press
Brookfield, Connecticut

A fishing boat slips from the harbor, chugging out to sea on the high tide.

Chug, chug, chug.

Trudge, trudge, trudge.

A colorful clam digger trudges past.
Pushes his bicycle onto the beach.

Bustling birds stand on the sand
waiting for the tide to drop.

Trudge, trudge, trudge.

Splash, splash, splash.

Out at sea, the fishing boat lowers its nets.

Hungry seagulls ride the waves, ready for the catch.

Splash, splash, splash.

Scratch, scratch, scratch.
The clam digger rakes the sand.
Mussels and clams
clattering, shattering into his bucket.
Scratch, scratch, scratch.

Kronk, kronk, kronk.

Lines of geese fly high
above the fishing boat,
dive down low over empty
boats on the shore.
The tide keeps dropping.

Kronk, kronk, kronk.

Prod, prod, prod.
Long beaks search for worms
while the tide is out.

Feet slap on wet sand.
Footprints gleaming.
Birdwatchers watching.

Prod, prod, prod.

Hush, hush, hush.

Crabs and starfish
hide quietly in
still rock pools.

Barnacles cling
to slippery rocks.
Green seaweed sparkles.
The tide is about to turn.

Hush, hush, hush.

Gush, gush, gush.
Gurgling water starts to
splash and crash over the rocks.
Birds dart and dash,
dodging invading waves
as the tide rushes in.

Gush,
gush, gush.

Swoop, swoop, swoop.

KL56

Gulls dive in to snatch,
grab, and gobble.
The heavy nets are
full of flapping fish.

SWOOP, swoop, swoop.

Stoop, stoop, stoop.

The clam digger leaves the beach,
his sacks full of shellfish.
Birds feed briskly
while the tide
races back
across the sand.

Stoop, stoop, stoop.

Beam, beam, beam.

The lighthouse shines, guiding the fishing boat past jagged rocks, back to the harbor and home on the high tide.

Beam, beam, beam.

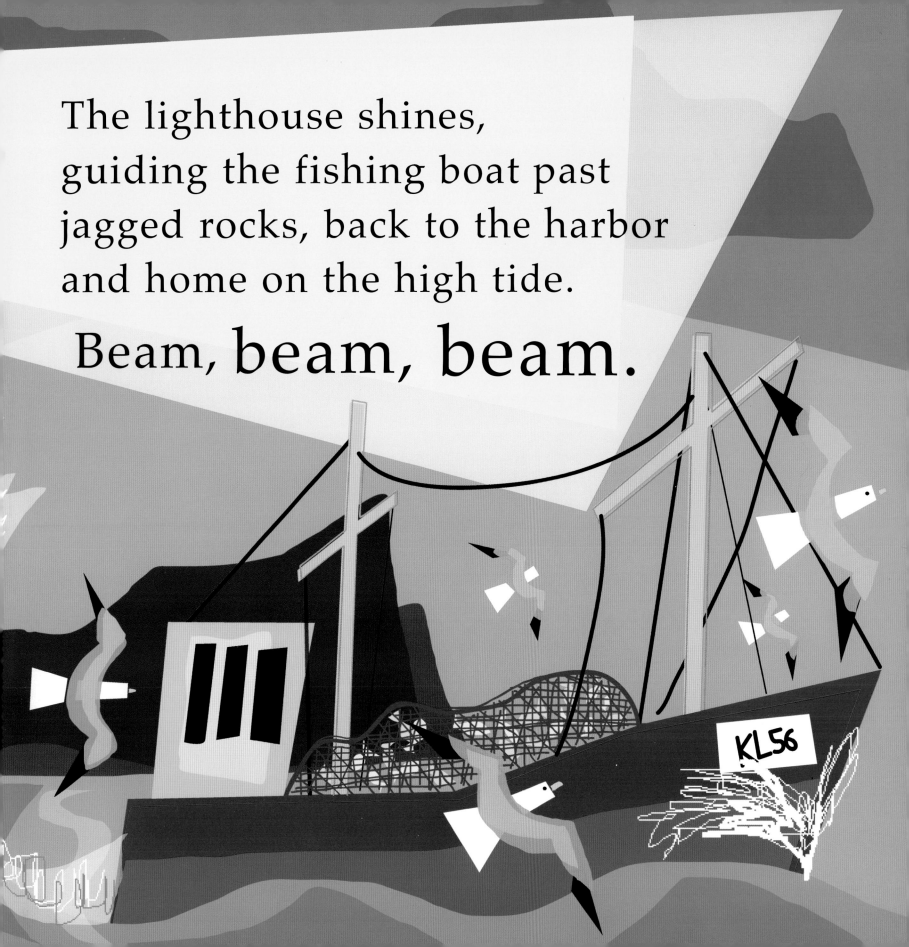

Chug. Trudge. Splash.
Scratch. Kronk. Prod.
Hush. Gush. Swoop.
Stoop. Beam. Gleam.

Gleam, gleam, gleam.

The day's catch glinting on the dock.
The little boat safe and sound,
ready for the next high tide.